For Heather -

with the best

of good wishes

from

Flora Gill Jacobs

July, 1981

# THE DOLL HOUSE MYSTERY

illustrated by Chuck Gruen

Coward-McCann, Inc.
New York

Ninth Impression

Library of Congress Catalog
Card Number: 58-7003

MANUFACTURED IN THE UNITED STATES OF AMERICA

For Betsy Grob (who named Priscilla)
and her brother Johnny

CONTENTS

*The characters — all but one — and events featured in this mystery are fictitious. Annie is a real character! The doll house, its furnishings, and its occupants are also real. The events themselves will have to take place in your imagination.*

THE
HOUSE
AND THE
OMEN

# ONE

The day the doll house arrived was as dreary as a day can be. Through the windows, Priscilla could see the streaks of rain falling steadily on the green, wet garden.

Although it was June (school was out for the summer), Mrs. Adams had lighted a small fire in the living-room fireplace, and Priscilla, Chubby, and Annie were as near to it as the brass fender would allow. Priscilla was nine and Chubby was five and Annie was three. Annie, although the youngest, was the only one of the three who could jump from the floor to the mantelpiece. The reason, perhaps, was that Priscilla and Chubby were children and Annie was a Siamese cat.

If you have never personally known any Siamese cats, you might as well be told that all of them are characters. It's not just that they look different from other cats, with their elegant cream-colored fur, their brown velvet trimmings and their beautiful blue eyes. They're a little crazy.

For instance: While the children were huddling about the fire, the doorbell rang. Priscilla ran to answer it, and Annie galloped madly around the living room, landing on every other chair and ending up on the mantelpiece. Only a Siamese, Tim said once, would go from first base to second by way of left field. Tim, the children's twelve-year-old brother, hardly ever said anything that didn't have baseball in it somewhere. Even if it didn't quite fit, Priscilla pointed out!

Priscilla opened the door. Lucy, her best friend, stood outside, her raincoat and umbrella dripping. "It's good you're here, Lucy," said Priscilla importantly. "The doll house is supposed to come in a little while!" Lucy took off her rubbers and came inside.

Annie walked over and carefully sniffed the

edge of Lucy's raincoat; when a few drops of water fell on her own coat, she galloped away.

"How do you know the doll house is coming?" Lucy asked, moving over to the fire.

"The delivery company told us," said Chubby. "They phoned and they told us." Chubby, who was a TV fan, pronounced his words very clearly and had an unusual vocabulary for a five-year old. He was thought to be terribly bright for his age and Priscilla said that some of the remarks Chubby made were so clever they positively frightened her.

Priscilla's plump little brother was noted also for eating — mostly cookies. Tim said Chubby could eat more cookies at one sitting than any other boy on the continent of North America.

"The doll house is an exact copy of our Great-aunt Eugenia's house, you know," said Chubby. "Perhaps you have seen our Great-aunt Eugenia's house. It is over on the other side of the city and we saw it once. We saw it from the outside. Great-aunt Eugenia was very eccentric — that means strange, Lucy — and she lived alone. We never met her. Nobody did. She died last month at the age of eighty-four. Her doll house was in the attic—"

"It was made for her when she was a little girl, to look like her house that she lived in," Priscilla interrupted. "It's hard to stop him once he gets started," she added in a haughty, big-sisterish voice. Chubby ignored her and went right on:

"Aunt Grace came from Philadelphia and found the doll house. She decided that Prilly would like it and —"

Everybody was so used to the way Chubby sometimes went on and on that nobody bothered to look surprised when he did. Priscilla again interrupted his speech.

"Great-aunt Eugenia's house is a very fancy-looking house," she said firmly. "It's a Victorian house. So this doll house is a Victorian doll house!"

"What kind is that?" Lucy asked.

"It's named after Queen Victoria," said Chubby, who couldn't read but never forgot anything anybody told him. He would have continued if Annie hadn't chosen this moment to leap onto the sofa, from the sofa to the curtain rod, and from the curtain rod to a tall chest. From this height, a foot from the ceiling, she bent around and casually washed her tail. She did all this to impress Lucy. Siamese cats are great showoffs and great jumpers and they like high places.

When Mrs. Adams came into the room with her knitting, though, Annie came down. Annie was interested in knitting.

"We were talking about Queen Victoria," Priscilla said.

"What do you know about Queen Victoria?" Mrs. Adams asked, giving a little tug at Priscilla's pale-yellow pony tail.

"Victoria was Queen of England," said Lucy, who was rather matter-of-fact.

"She was very small," said Priscilla, who liked unusual bits of information.

"She invented Victorian doll houses," said Chubby, who sometimes had to invent *his* information. Though often impressive, this wasn't always accurate.

"No, Chubby," Mrs. Adams corrected. "That's not quite right. She didn't invent them. She was queen for such a long time that many things were named after her. She reigned a great part of the last century and, during that time, a fancy kind of furniture began to be used. The chairs had lots of stuffing and the wood had lots of carving."

Annie, unnoticed by anyone, was crouched under the wing chair getting ready to take Mrs. Adams' ball of red yarn by surprise. Siamese cats are mad about red.

"People collected all sorts of little objects — china dogs and vases and things — and stood them around on shelves," Mrs. Adams continued. "I remember visiting in Great-aunt Eugenia's house when I was a little girl. It was crammed with furniture and bric-a-brac. It's a good thing those houses had high ceilings and big rooms or people could hardly have breathed."

Just then Annie, who had taken about five minutes to pounce on the ball of yarn, pounced. She liked to take things by surprise. This ball of yarn was positively astonished. "Oh, dear!" cried Mrs. Adams, as Annie carried it off, trailing red wool clear across the hall and into the dining room.

At that moment the doorbell rang. There was a certain amount of shrieking and running about while Mrs. Adams grabbed the wool and Priscilla went to answer the door. Annie gave her customary doorbell performance, racing after Priscilla like a small pony.

Priscilla opened the door. "It's the doll house!" she shouted. "The doll house is here!" Standing on the porch, next to the wettest delivery man Priscilla had ever seen, was a huge shape covered with a piece of soggy canvas.

Next to the huge, wet canvas, as though it were part of the shipment, its fur all matted with the rain, sat a strange black cat. Even in her excitement, Priscilla noticed its unfriendly yellow eyes.

"Package for Miss Priscilla Adams," the delivery man announced. Priscilla thought "package" a funny word to describe what had arrived. She signed the slip with pride — it was the first she had ever signed. Just as she dotted the final *i*, there was a great clap of thunder. She nearly dropped the pencil.

Some people might have said it was an omen. Whether it was or not (and most people don't believe in omens), the thunderclap, the rainy, dreary day, and the strange black cat seemed to set the stage for some exceedingly mysterious events which were to follow.

A
DISTURBING
PHONE
CALL

# TWO

When the delivery man hauled the soggy canvas off the doll house, Priscilla and Lucy and Chubby said "Oh!" in a chorus. Chubby clapped his hand to his head and opened his mouth very wide.

Priscilla couldn't say another word for at least a minute. "It *does* look just like Great-aunt Eugenia's house!" she declared finally. "I remember the time we drove past it."

Tim hadn't bothered to be present when the doll house arrived. Priscilla would have suspected that he was off playing second base somewhere, if anyone ever played baseball in such weather. However, just as the delivery man drove away, Tim appeared. He was drenched with rain but he wasn't too wet to be impressed. He whistled. Tim always whistled when he was impressed. He helped Mabel, the Adams' maid, carry the doll house up to Priscilla's room.

They set it on a low table. Priscilla hadn't dreamed it would be so large. It was about four feet tall and four feet wide and seemed to take up half her room. It was a strange-looking doll house, Priscilla thought to herself, though she wouldn't have dreamed of admitting such a thing out loud. It reminded her of another house — suddenly she remembered which house. It reminded her of the old, empty Burton house at the end of the bus line — the house that everybody said was haunted.

"Look at all the funny windows," Lucy said.

"They're real glass," said Priscilla. The windows *were* unusual. They were tall and narrow to match the tall, narrow rooms. Among them were four bay windows which stood away from the imitation brownstone walls like little glassed-in balconies.

Chubby pushed in an upstairs window. "Chubby, what have you done?" Priscilla complained.

"Nothing," Chubby said. "These windows are casement windows. They're on hinges and they're supposed to swing in."

Chubby's family was used to him, but everyone was impressed. "That child is a genius," Priscilla said. "Where did you learn that?"

"On Channel Seven," said Chubby matter-of-factly.

"Look at these windows around the door," Lucy said. "Red and dark blue!"

"Those are called stained-glass windows," Mrs. Adams explained. "That's the colored kind of glass that's used in churches. In Victorian days people often had it in their houses, too." There were dormer windows in the attic — little short windows that stuck out from the roof.

Something occurred to Priscilla. "How many rooms does it have?" she suddenly demanded. "How do you get inside it?"

Tim, having helped to carry it upstairs, had special knowledge. "The back opens on hinges," he said.

Everybody rushed around to the back. Mrs. Adams unfastened the latches and the back swung open. The children almost cheered when the inside was revealed — it looked so like a real house. Even Tim joined in the general excitement. Then, embarrassed at having shown so much interest in a doll house, he turned away, pounding a fist into his fielder's glove, which he just happened to have with him. He didn't leave, though.

There were eight rooms, an attic, and a staircase. There were designs painted on the ceilings and little carved doors with brass knobs leading from room to room. Velvet carpeted the floors, red in some rooms and green in others. Priscilla noticed that it all had a queer, interesting, musty smell.

Chubby was so excited that his cowlick practically stood on end. "Is that the kitchen?" he wanted to know, pointing to a room with a checkered floor. Everybody laughed because there was Chubby thinking about food as usual.

Mrs. Adams made a discovery. "Look at the

little scorch marks on these walls!" she said. "There must have been little wall sconces with candles that somebody lighted. But don't let that give you any ideas, girls," she added quickly. "This doll house is old and dry and might easily catch on fire."

"Anyway it has electric lights," Lucy remarked. This was another discovery and caused much excitement. Chubby found a tightly coiled cord and plug at one side of the doll house. When Priscilla plugged it in, the lights went on.

"These must have been added in later years," Mrs. Adams said. "But even that must have been a long time ago and it's lucky they still work."

Tim put down his fielder's glove to walk over and peer in. "It looks sort of creepy to me," he said.

Priscilla shivered. "What a mean thing to say! It's a fine doll house!" She was trying not to admit to herself that it did look a bit gloomy.

They moved to the front of the house. Little lanterns with real wicks stood on either side of the front door.

"These could really be lighted, with a little kerosene," said Mrs. Adams. "But they are very old and you must promise me not to do it. It would be dangerous!"

"This is sure a dangerous doll house," Tim said.

"That will be enough of that, Tim," Mrs. Adams warned. She pointed out to the other children that the lanterns each had a tiny wheel to raise or lower the flame.

Suddenly, from behind the doll house, there came a fearsome growling. It was strangely familiar, but startling. Priscilla and Chubby rushed to the back of the doll house, quickly followed by the others. In the drawing room, Annie stood, her lovely cream-colored fur with its brown trimming beautiful against the green carpet. Her back was arched and her tail puffed out about three inches. For a minute or so they just stood and watched her. Her growling, which was almost like a low moan, continued, and she sniffed anxiously at doll-house walls, carpet, and ceiling. Her beautiful blue eyes blinked in bewilderment as all the faces stared in at her.

"She's afraid of the doll house!" Chubby pointed out.

"I wonder why?" said Priscilla anxiously.

"Like I said," said Tim, but not very loudly.

Mrs. Adams frowned at Tim and then said, "I guess Mabel let her in. We put her on the porch while Mabel and Tim carried the doll house upstairs." Mothers never take mysterious things very seriously. Mrs. Adams hauled Annie out of the doll house and tossed her gently to the floor.

Annie's mood changed instantly. She stopped growling and began to complain. "Maiyou, aiyou, wow, wo-ow," she declared in loud, aggrieved tones. A Siamese cat's voice, by the way, is deep, rich, and expressive. Annie howled in a loud throaty voice when she wanted something, and she usually got it. She didn't get the doll house, though. However much it frightened her, she obviously wanted it, to judge by her complaints when she was removed. Following these remarks, she went with great dignity to the other end of the room and sat down, folding herself together neatly and turning her back on all of them.

Once, when Annie was just a kitten, she had been discovered rolling merrily on her back on the mantelpiece clutching a little china figurine — a figure of a little girl. She had complained when this was taken away from her. The figurine had to be hidden in a drawer till Annie "grew up." As Mrs. Adams said, Annie was very stubborn.

Anybody could see that it was going to be quite a project to get Priscilla's doll house away from Annie if she decided she liked it.

"It's not so bad as long as there's no furniture," Priscilla said. "But can you picture her in there with tables and chairs?"

"Where *are* the tables and chairs?" Lucy asked. This reminded the children that in their excitement they had neglected three interesting-looking boxes packed inside the doll-house attic.

Priscilla set to work on these at once and there were fine noises of paper tearing and cardboard crunching. Annie stopped sulking and came over to have a look. Paper and string are lovely toys to a Siamese cat.

There were dozens of tiny packages fastened with rubber bands or string, and small, oddly shaped, tissue-wrapped objects. Just as Priscilla was about to open the first one, the phone rang, and Mrs. Adams went down the hall to the study to answer it.

"We'll wait till you get back, Mother," said Priscilla, though she was just dying to begin. Then she remembered that the scissors in the study might be helpful to snip some of the string, and she followed her mother down the hall.

Mrs. Adams had picked up the phone and was explaining to Cousin Julia that they were in the midst of unpacking Aunt Eugenia's doll-house furnishings and she'd call back if Cousin Julia didn't mind.

As Priscilla was returning to her room, she heard another bit of her mother's conversation. "Yes, poor Aunt Eugenia," said Mrs. Adams.

"Living in that big old house with all those ghosts!"

Priscilla stopped still. Was Aunt Eugenia's house a haunted house, too? Like the Burton house at the end of the bus line?

Then the phone conversation was ended, and Priscilla and her mother were back in front of the doll house with heaps of tiny packages spread before them. Priscilla had no time to think about ghosts.

Impatient Annie had begun ripping the tissue off one of the packages, and the shape of a little upholstered chair was plainly visible. Suddenly Annie stopped playing with the wrappings and sat bolt upright. She seemed to be listening. Then she arched her back and growled. At that moment everybody heard a sort of unearthly howl. It didn't sound quite real.

"What was that?" said Priscilla, alarmed.

"What was it, Annie, old girl?" said Tim. He had sat bolt upright, too. Just then Mr. Adams, who had arrived from his office a few moments before, came upstairs. "Where did that strange-looking black cat outside come from?" he asked. "It tried to run past me into the house. And what's it howling about?"

Then he noticed the doll house.

"By George!" said Mr. Adams. "That's a fine, gloomy Victorian house if ever I saw one!"

"Gloomy, Daddy?" Priscilla said anxiously.

"Have I said the wrong thing?" Daddy demanded. "It's a *terrific* doll house!" The children started to point out its wonders. Everyone forgot about the howling cat outside.

THE
HOUSE
OF
SHADOW

## THREE

"Shall we take turns opening, Mother?" Priscilla suggested.

This was thought to be a fine idea and everyone joined in, even Tim and Chubby. Priscilla opened the first piece. It was a beautiful little table with a marble top. "Why, it's real marble," said Mrs. Adams. "People had marble tops all over the place in those days. And they've become fashionable again."

Lucy unpacked a plump, upholstered drawing-room set, piece by piece. It was red velvet with curvy wood trimming.

Chubby opened a package which contained a little iron stove and decided he'd just bake his own cookies from now on. The stove had a door that really opened and you could put little pieces of wood in it. It also had a stovepipe. Priscilla had been putting some of the furniture on the big table which held the doll house, but she placed this fine stove right in the kitchen.

Tim's package revealed a wall telephone, the kind people used about 1880. Tim turned the little metal crank and the bell on top rang! After that he didn't even look at his baseball glove for at least an hour.

It was Mrs. Adams who unpacked the brass chandeliers. One had holders that birthday candles just fitted into, and another, meant to look like a gas lamp, had beautiful little glass shades.

They unwrapped and unwrapped: A tiny china tea set, desks and cupboards, a little piano with a stool that really revolved, pictures in fancy brass frames, a sewing machine with a needle that went up and down when you turned the wheel.

When they came to the box of doll-house dolls, Priscilla was practically delirious! There was even a butler, a proper one with sideburns. And a maid with a feather duster and the neatest braided hairdo of real-looking hair. There was a baby in a buggy with a parasol top. There was a little boy in a sailor suit, a little girl with a china doll, and a small dark-faced doll with a black wig and a red dress who looked rather Mexican. There was also a French pastry cook in a tall chef's hat and a dainty lady with the tiniest bunch of keys at her waist.

"I think she's meant to be the housekeeper," said Priscilla. She was placing the lady next to the marble-topped buffet in the dining room when she saw something she hadn't noticed before inside the metal fender of the built-in fireplace. It seemed to be a little card with printing on it. She managed, with a little tugging, to pull it out.

"What is it, Prilly?" Lucy asked.

Priscilla had a sort of strange expression on her face.

"Read it, Prilly," said Chubby, who noticed that there was lettering on the card. Brilliant as he was, he could read only a few carefully selected words such as *food, pie,* and *cake.*

Priscilla looked again at the first sentence, printed in ink in tall, faded letters. Then she read in a voice that she hoped sounded ordinary: "This is the House of Shadow." She read the second line in a voice so low that Chubby asked her to repeat it:

"INTRUDERS BEWARE!"

The only other line was *"Enter at own risk."*

"Well, that's not a very friendly attitude," said Mrs. Adams brightly. Mothers have a way of making the most extraordinary things sound ordinary.

"I have to go tell Mabel about dinner," she added. "I think you've opened just about everything." Tim also left the room. He had had enough of doll houses for one day.

Priscilla was trying not to think about the message on the strange card. She fished around in the bottom of the boxes to make sure nothing was left in the debris. It was fortunate she did, because there were two small packages she had missed.

One was a little umbrella stand with three very gay umbrellas.

And one was a black cat!

"It looks something like the one we saw on the porch," Lucy said. Priscilla didn't say anything.

The cat's "fur" even looked matted, she thought, and when she first touched the cat, she had the oddest sensation. It felt wet as though *it* had been out in the rain! However, it was made of painted metal and perhaps it felt cold rather than wet, as metal often does.

Something else about the cat was strange, though. It had yellow eyes. This wasn't unusual, but they seemed to Priscilla *unfriendly* yellow eyes.

Chubby chose that moment to wander off, probably in search of cookies, and Priscilla and Lucy were left alone.

Priscilla picked up the little card. "What do *you* think, Lucy?" she asked significantly.

"Think of what?" Lucy said. Really, sometimes, Lucy didn't seem very bright. Priscilla decided to tell Lucy about her mother's phone conversation with Cousin Julia.

"You know what I'm beginning to think?" Priscilla finished. "I'm beginning to think this doll house is haunted, too!"

"Do you think it has miniature ghosts in it?" Lucy said casually. Lucy was *so* matter-of-fact, Priscilla thought. Actually this was meant to be a joke, and it was rather a good one for Lucy. She was disappointed when Priscilla didn't laugh.

Just as Priscilla was about to place the black cat on the hearth rug in the doll-house bedroom, Annie growled and arched her back. They heard the strange, loud cry outside which they had heard before. It sounded very loud. And *very* strange. Even Lucy shivered a little. The miniature black cat dropped from Priscilla's hand.

THE
MYSTERY
THICKENS

## FOUR

After dinner that evening, Priscilla and Lucy finished arranging the furniture in the doll house. Lucy was spending the night in honor of the occasion. It was still pouring rain outdoors and thundering ominously from time to time. A good dinner, though, had chased away some of Priscilla's forebodings, despite the gloomy weather.

They had a marvelous time arranging the doll household, even though both Chubby and Annie insisted on helping. Priscilla and Chubby had a small argument about Monsieur Chocolat, which was the name Priscilla had given the little French pastry cook. Priscilla had placed him in the dining room where, she declared, the housekeeper was giving him instructions about making a batch of cream puffs. Chubby insisted that he belonged in the kitchen. He grabbed M. Chocolat out of Priscilla's hand. Priscilla grabbed him out of Chubby's hand. Monsieur's white apron got somewhat smudged. This wasn't surprising when you consider that Chubby had been having a bedtime snack of seven molasses cookies a few minutes before.

"Chadwell Adams!" Priscilla screamed. Chadwell was Chubby's real name and calling him by it was the crowning insult. Chubby started to yell, partly perhaps because Priscilla pinched him.

Mrs. Adams, who overheard the commotion all the way from the study, came in and made peace. Chubby could watch, she ruled, but this was Priscilla's doll house and Priscilla was to decide where pastry cooks or furniture should be placed.

Chubby, with a tear-streaked face, sat solemnly a few feet away while the project continued, but Annie's offers of help couldn't be spurned so easily. She spent most of her time either jumping on

Priscilla's shoulder in an attempt to get into the doll house, or rolling over.

When Annie rolled over, with her chin outstretched and her paws stuck daintily in the air, whoever was nearest was supposed to come pet her. People were continually having to get up out of their chairs to do this because Annie, alas, was very spoiled and kept screaming at them till they did as she wished.

After Priscilla and Lucy had arranged the furniture, they turned off all the lights in Priscilla's room except the ones in the doll house and stood back to admire the effect.

"Look at the light coming through the stained glass!" Priscilla remarked. "Doesn't Amanda look real standing by the bedroom window?"

Tim came into the room. "You still fooling with that thing?" he said. Tim couldn't fool Priscilla, though — he was interested in the doll house more than he would admit. Tim didn't come into Priscilla's room very often. There were no autographed baseballs in it.

He went over, very casually, and looked in at the back. "It's spooky with the lights on," he said.

"Please stop saying things like that," said Priscilla angrily. "It's a beautiful doll house." Sometimes people will think things themselves but they get very cross when other people mention them.

At that moment there was a tremendous clap of thunder. It was followed by the strange cry, which seemed to pierce the very walls of the Adams' house.

"See what I mean?" said Tim. Leering at the girls, he left the room.

"Does Tim think this doll house has ghosts in it?" said Chubby in a loud, clear, hopeful voice. He seemed to be recovered from his quarrel with Priscilla.

"Tim is just talking, Chubby," said Priscilla. "He doesn't mean a thing." While she was saying these brave words, Priscilla was trying not to notice that the doll house cast strange shadows on the wall at night, and that the lighting *was* sort of gloomy.

Mrs. Adams came up the stairs and stopped at Priscilla's door. "There's milk and some buns on the kitchen table, girls, and you should be going to bed soon."

"For me, too?" said Chubby.

He was ushered down the hall by his mother personally, with Annie as a sort of escort. Annie never could resist attacking feet without shoes on them, and she was after Chubby's pajama feet.

"You know you should have been in bed an hour ago," Mrs. Adams said firmly.

After carefully fastening the back of the doll house so that Annie couldn't get into it, the two girls went down to the kitchen.

When they returned fifteen minutes later, the double doors at the front of the house were swung open. Crouched inside the hall looking proudly out was Miss Annie. She acted as though she had built the doll house herself and planned to spend the rest of her days in it — perhaps just where she was. She had a rather silly expression on her face.

Priscilla tried to pull her out. She wouldn't pull. She dug in with her claws and just stayed. She had puffed herself up to fit inside the hall and she practically reached the ceiling. The little umbrella stand lay on its side beneath a silky paw, its contents scattered on the hall carpet.

"I guess she's not afraid of the doll house any more," said Priscilla. "That *was* strange, though, wasn't it?"

"Oh, you know how cats are," Lucy replied. Lucy wasn't much better at mysteries than somebody's mother.

Priscilla looked at her with a disappointed expression. She took her hands out of the doll house a minute, to think. Annie took the opportunity to scrunch through the hall door into the dining room.

"Annie!" Priscilla yelled.

"You wouldn't think she could get through that narrow little door," she added. "She's made just like an accordion or a folding chair — I forget which."

Lucy looked through a dining-room window. "She's hardly knocked anything down at all."

Priscilla looked through another window, on the side. "That silly cat is just standing there," she said. "Well, there's only one thing to do." Priscilla unhinged the back of the doll house. She reached in for Annie and started to lift her out, but Annie had other ideas. She resisted. Priscilla, trying to pull her out, was knocking over furniture right and left. She let go. Annie went back through the dining-room door into the front hall and put her paws on the stair landing. Nothing on the second floor had been touched and Priscilla wanted to keep it that way. She didn't know what she was going to do. Fortunately, at that moment the Adams' doorbell rang. Answering the door was part of Annie's work. She wriggled through the double doors, jumped to the floor, and dashed for the stairs.

"Who could that be at this hour?" Priscilla heard her mother say. Mr. and Mrs. Adams were

in the upstairs sitting room. Mr. Adams went downstairs to answer the bell.

Mrs. Adams had come out into the hall. "I can't imagine on a night like this—"

Everybody listened as Mr. Adams opened the door. "No, George," they heard him say. "I don't know. We heard it, too." Nobody could catch what George Greely, the man who lived next door, was saying, though they recognized his voice.

"Won't you come in out of the rain?" Mr. Greely evidently refused. The two talked for a couple of minutes and the girls heard Mr. Adams say "good-night" and bolt the door.

When he came upstairs, Lucy and Priscilla surrounded him and demanded to know what Mr. Greely had wanted. "It's just that strange cat we've been hearing," Mr. Adams said. "The Greelys have been hearing it, too. George thought it might be sick or injured and went out to look for it. But he hasn't been able to catch sight of it."

"Oh, Daddy," said Priscilla, looking very unhappy. Priscilla was very sympathetic to animals, and she couldn't bear to think of one being out in such a storm. She was also confused. She didn't know whether she felt sympathetic about this animal or not. This cat was so strange.

Mr. Adams assured Priscilla that cats were very good at taking care of themselves. Besides, she had a cat problem of her own, right in the house. So she stopped worrying about the strange cat. She and Lucy went to bed.

After a great deal of conversation about the events of the evening, the girls finally fell asleep. Priscilla was dreaming about the doll house: The housemaid was dusting. The little girl was playing with her doll. The housekeeper was opening cupboards with her keys. And the butler was buttling.

Suddenly Priscilla was wide awake. She looked over at the doll house. Lights seemed to be flashing in the dining room. Strange little noises seemed to be coming from the doll house. None of them sounded as strange, though, as a noise outside the Adams' house. The black cat was howling again.

TIM
ADAMS,
PRIVATE
DETECTIVE

# FIVE

Priscilla sat straight up. "Lucy," she whispered.

Lucy didn't wake immediately. Priscilla finally had to tug at her sheet.

"What — is it?" Lucy asked sleepily.

"The doll house —" said Priscilla. "Look!"

"What's the matter with it?" Lucy yawned.

"There are funny lights in it," said Priscilla. "And noises."

"I don't see any lights," Lucy said, and she turned over to go back to sleep. A particularly loud clap of thunder brought her half awake again. "Is that the noise?" she said.

" 'Course not," Priscilla murmured. Conversation had given her courage. She slipped out of bed.

She was halfway across the room when she heard a sort of odd thud and then a thump, and she realized that the flashing lights from the doll house had stopped. A different sort of light filled Priscilla's room. Through her window there was a blaze of lightning, followed by a roll of thunder, and this frightened Priscilla so that she rushed over to turn on her bed lamp. She stumbled over a footstool and had a time locating the light switch, but at last she reached the switch and turned on the lamp.

This seemed to reveal more shadows than light. Priscilla approached the doll house with her heart beating so loudly that she couldn't tell if she still heard noises there or not.

The back of the doll house was open! Some furniture was scattered about. Then Priscilla remembered that, in all the confusion before going to bed, she hadn't fastened the back, and had never straightened the furniture which Annie had knocked over in the scuffle. Priscilla had been really tired; she was usually an orderly girl. Now

she forgot that she was frightened and began carefully to restore the furnishings to their proper places.

It was when Priscilla had put the last piece in order that she realized the little dark-faced doll with the black wig whom she had named Amanda had disappeared. Priscilla particularly remembered how real Amanda had looked standing in her red dress by the bedroom window. She remembered that the upstairs hadn't been upset at all in the scramble with Annie.

What seemed strangest to her, though, was that the black metal cat was *not* on the hearth rug in the doll-house bedroom where she had carefully placed him. He was in front of the doll house staring up at her!

Priscilla's heart, which had quieted down, began to beat rapidly again. Maybe Tim was right, she decided. Maybe this *was* a strange doll house! She didn't even dare think of her own fears about it — her mother's remark about ghosts to Cousin Julia — or the card about the House of Shadow.

Priscilla decided not to try to wake Lucy again. The bedroom door was ajar, and she pushed it open and went out into the hall. She went to Tim's third-floor room and tapped at his partly open door.

Tim was better at waking than Lucy. He was up in a flash. Priscilla quickly whispered what had happened. Tim was delighted. Maybe he was right about the doll house, after all. Besides, this was just the kind of adventure he liked. Although it *was* sort of queer. Like Priscilla's, his heart began to beat a little faster, though he would never have admitted it.

They crept down the stairs. Annie, who usually slept at the foot of Tim's bed, joined them as they entered Priscilla's room.

They tiptoed over to the doll house, Tim carrying his Boy Scout flashlight and a magnifying glass. What he intended to do with the glass neither Priscilla nor Tim himself quite knew. But to Priscilla, even in his pajamas, he looked for all the world like Sherlock Holmes.

The little dark-faced doll had most certainly vanished. Tim peered into every room through his magnifying glass, which seemed, after all, very useful for the purpose. Then he agreed that Amanda was gone.

"If I had one of those fingerprint outfits, it might help," Tim announced. There seemed to be an absence of clues. This is sometimes embarrassing to a detective.

"There's a bigger magnifying glass on the desk in the study," he remarked finally. "I'll go get it." Priscilla followed him out into the hall — it seemed less mysterious out there.

Tim returned with the large magnifying glass and they started back into the bedroom.

Priscilla gasped. "Look!" she said softly. "The lights again! See — two of them in the upstairs bedroom!"

Tim saw them, too. They *were* strange, and they seemed to flash as Priscilla had said. "They look like diamonds," he whispered. "Except they're sort of red at the same time."

He and Priscilla crept over to the house. Tim bravely looked into the bedroom — you had to be brave just to look — and there was Annie!

The ridiculous puss rolled over when she saw her friends, sending chairs and beds in odd directions.

"For Pete's sake!" said Tim with relief, but with disappointment, too.

Priscilla felt ashamed. "I forgot that her eyes sometimes look like that in the dark," she said. "And I think I heard when the black cat fell onto the table. And that thump must have been when Annie jumped down."

A little late, Tim now located a clue. "With this big magnifying glass," he said, "you can see her fur all over everything."

"She likes red," Priscilla reminded him. "That's probably why she selected Amanda."

"What's going on in here?" a new voice inquired. It was Mrs. Adams, finally awakened by the unusual footsteps and noises.

Tim gave her a brief description of what had happened. Annie, standing knee-deep in Victorian doll-house furniture in the bedroom, and looking very proud of herself, didn't have too much to add. "Aiyou," she said.

Priscilla had a sudden thought. "What do you suppose she did with Amanda?"

"You can look for Amanda in the morning, dear," Mrs. Adams said pleasantly.

"Oh, no, Mother," said Priscilla, shocked. "I can't possibly go to sleep till I find Amanda!"

Tim, with further detective work to do, brightened. Taking his magnifying glass and flashlight, he started down the stairs. "You might do better with this, Tim," said Mrs. Adams, snapping on the hall light.

It spoiled the fun but it served the purpose. At the fourth step from the bottom, poor Amanda lay just where her kidnaper had left her.

Priscilla welcomed her with open hands but was shocked by her appearance. Her poor little black wig was somewhat disarranged — probably by little cat teeth. Her red dress looked a bit chewed up, too.

"You *bad* kitty!" said Priscilla severely to the guilty party, who jumped casually from the doll-house bedroom to the floor and fled wisely from the room.

Tim said good night and went back upstairs. Mrs. Adams tucked Priscilla into bed. "Is anything the matter?" said Lucy. She was finally awake!

(Thereafter, the doll house was carefully closed when it was not being played with. The back was latched, and a paper clip hooked across the two knobs on the double doors at the front of the house held them fast.)

Everyone slept well that night, thinking the mystery was ended. Only the black cat, huddling under a rhododendron bush in the garden beneath Priscilla's window, may have known better . . . .

MINIATURE
GHOSTS?

# SIX

At breakfast the next morning, there was a good deal of cheerful conversation about Amanda's kid-naping. The sun had finally come out. Moreover, the mysterious black cat had stopped howling and seemed to have vanished.

Everyone was busy eating waffles with straw-berry jam when Chubby looked up very seriously and gave an opinion. "If Prilly had called me to solve the mystery instead of Tim, do you know what?" he said.

"What?" Chubby's father replied politely.

"Well, you know that butler," said Chubby, chin-deep in jam. "I'd have bet it was the butler. On television it is lots of times."

"Yes," Mrs. Adams said. "What's the use of having a perfectly splendid doll-house butler if you can't blame the mystery on him?"

"But Chubby," Priscilla protested. "Underwood didn't do it. Annie did it." Underwood was the name Priscilla had given the butler. Her father's typewriter was an Underwood and it seemed a good name for a butler, somehow.

"Chubb should read some whodunits," said Tim.

"Who done what?" said Chubby, who knew perfectly well that whodunits are mystery stories of a certain kind.

"That isn't very good grammar," said Lucy, who, as usual, was being very matter-of-fact.

"That's what they call crime stories, silly," said Tim, who wasn't too fond of Lucy.

"A crime is like what Annie committed last night," said Priscilla, though no one had asked her. "Doing away with Amanda."

Chubby was determined to continue with his

theory. Well, if the butler hadn't done it, he said, then maybe M. Chocolat would have been the one.

Nobody said anything when Chubby mentioned the pastry *cook*. The joke about Chubby and food was getting a little used up. Besides, Priscilla hadn't quite got over her squabble with Chubby about M. Chocolat the evening before.

"Anyway, it was Annie," Priscilla said again. She didn't share Chubby's interest in the latest detective methods. The matter dropped. Everyone — perhaps even Chubby himself — was more interested in waffles.

It was a busy day for the doll house. There were a few chairs to be reglued and things of that sort. Amanda, recovering from her terrible experience, was tucked into the canopied bed all day and was brought breakfast, lunch, and tea. She had her strength back after that and was permitted to fend for herself for dinner.

The Adams' own dinner that night was very satisfactory — lamb chops and baked potatoes — till Tim mentioned that he had seen the strange black cat outside on his way in. That bothered Priscilla. She didn't quite know why since she had seen how groundless fears could be, but she didn't say anything. Lucy had gone home. Even a best friend can't stay overnight forever.

"I've asked Kay Smithers to sit tonight while we visit the Morrises," said Mrs. Adams.

"I'm going to sleep at Pete's," Tim announced, having got permission earlier. He nearly always made it his business to be away from home when there was a baby sitter. At the age of twelve, he considered a sitter an insult to his ability to handle any problem which might arise. (He felt that, on the whole, he had managed Amanda's case in great style.)

There was silence for a moment or two, suddenly broken by an alarming wail. The black cat was indeed back again. Priscilla sighed. She wished Tim weren't going to be at Pete's. She didn't like Kay Smithers very much; Kay was seventeen and was going to college next year, and she was stuck-up. If anything came up like about Amanda,

Priscilla knew she wouldn't call Kay to come as she had called Tim.

When Priscilla went to bed, she sort of wished that Lucy had stayed. True, Lucy hadn't been much help in an emergency the night before, but somehow Lucy asleep was better than no Lucy at all. Besides, Lucy never imagined anything. There was some benefit to being plain matter-of-fact. Priscilla, on the other hand, imagined all sorts of things. Once she thought she saw ghosts in the back yard beneath her bedroom window — about seven ghosts doing a strange, slow dance. They had turned out to be some towels Mabel had left on the line by mistake.

Mrs. Adams had suggested that Priscilla close her door so that Annie couldn't even try to get into the doll house. Priscilla closed it carefully, after making certain that Annie wasn't in her room. Then she said her prayers, got into bed, and went off to sleep.

A little later — it's hard to tell how much later when you've been asleep — she suddenly woke.

The cat was howling outside, low, but somehow even more strangely than usual. It didn't quite sound like a cat. In fact, it didn't really sound like anything Priscilla had ever heard.

She looked quickly toward the doll house. It was a black night; there was no rain, but there was no moon either, and she couldn't see a thing. Suddenly she heard the doll house creak on its table. Little scraping noises seemed to be coming from inside!

Priscilla held her breath a moment or two and listened. It was impossible to know what to do. She was determined not to call Kay Smithers. She didn't want to turn on her light. She was almost afraid to see!

A moment or two passed. Priscilla heard strange, soft footsteps coming toward her bed. Then, suddenly, the steps were going toward her bedroom door which seemed to be open. How had it opened?

The sound of the steps went slowly through the door and started down the hall. Priscilla switched on her light and was out of bed in one bound. She rushed out into the hall. If anyone had been there, though, there was no one to be seen now.

Priscilla walked back to the study. There was always a lamp lighted there. It was usually a cozy-looking room, but at the moment even the study didn't look friendly. Then Priscilla noticed Annie curled up in the green leather chair, shading her eyes with her tail as she did when she was fast asleep. She removed it to look at Priscilla and gave a big yawn.

Priscilla had a sudden thought. Although Annie looked as though she had been genuinely asleep, you couldn't count on it. Maybe the doll house had been left open accidentally and Annie had paid it another visit. This thought gave Priscilla courage. She rushed back to her room and over to the doll house. It was shut tight!

She began to feel uneasy again. She decided to open the doll house and see how things looked inside.

When Priscilla unhinged the back and turned on the lights, their rather dim glow cast strange shadows on the wall. She first glanced over to where Amanda stood by the bedroom window. She was just where she was supposed to be. Everything seemed in place. Priscilla started to turn off the lights and close the house when something made her look into the dining room.

Mrs. Biggs, the housekeeper, was standing by the marble-topped sideboard where she was giving those instructions about cream puffs to M. Chocolat. But where was Monsieur? Priscilla looked in every room. The little pastry cook was not in the house!

Priscilla knew M. Chocolat had been in his place shortly before she went to bed. She had been playing with the doll house for nearly an hour. Suddenly she remembered something else. She had placed the black cat next to the housekeeper. The cat was supposed to be rubbing at the housekeeper's skirt. There was no black cat rubbing against it.

The cat — for some reason, Priscilla had given it no name — had disappeared, too.

Lucy's words came back to Priscilla. Could there be — miniature ghosts?

Priscilla rushed out into the hall. She was crying a little. Kay Smithers must have heard. "Is everything all right up there?"

Priscilla didn't answer. She sat down on the top step to wait for her mother and father. Hearing no further sound, Kay Smithers didn't come to investigate.

THE
STRANGE
CASE
OF
THE
PASTRYCOOK

# SEVEN

Priscilla was asleep at the top of the stairs, her head resting uneasily against the banister, when her father and mother came home and found her there. Annie was snuggled close to Priscilla's right knee.

Although Mr. and Mrs. Adams were mystified, they decided not to wake her. Priscilla's father picked her up gently and carried her off to her bed. While her mother was covering her, Priscilla stirred a little and began to say something.

"You'll tell us in the morning, darling," said her mother. Priscilla was too nearly asleep to protest.

It must have been an hour later when she woke with a start. For a moment Priscilla thought she was still on the stairs. She didn't know exactly where she was. The house was very still and dark. When Priscilla realized what had happened, she knew that her parents must now themselves be asleep.

A board in the floor squeaked. Then Priscilla heard the softly thumping steps again, followed by sounds of the doll house being unfastened. The doll-house table was creaking. Priscilla was terrified. It was too much for one night. She nearly screamed, but she was too frightened even to whisper. Instead she drew the sheet up to her neck and just listened. There were a few strange, scraping noises; then a sound as though the doll house were being latched.

A moment passed. The quiet steps began again. They were coming close to Priscilla's bed.

She could hear breathing. Then, just when the steps came closest, again they seemed to turn and go through the door into the hall. Almost immediately there was a dreadful scream!

For a moment Priscilla wondered if she were the one who had screamed. Then she realized that the noise came from the hall. She heard a door open and her father's reassuring voice. "What's going on out here?"

The hall light was switched on. Priscilla bounded out of bed and into the hall. The screaming continued; it was practically deafening.

A strange sight met Priscilla's eyes. Chubby was standing in the middle of the hall, yelling at the top of his lungs. Annie was clutching one of his pajama feet firmly between her teeth.

"What can have got into Annie?" Mrs. Adams said. She bent over to pull Annie away. "Do let go! Bad kitty!"

Annie didn't seem to want to let go. Priscilla's father had to command her to do so. Then instead of rushing away as she generally did when she misbehaved, she stayed there, looking rather pleased with herself. In fact, she rolled over.

Mrs. Adams tried to soothe Chubby. "What

happened, dear?" she said. "What are you doing out here in the hall?"

Chubby's screaming changed into a spell of terrible weeping. He seemed to be trying to explain something, but he was crying so loudly that nobody could make out a word.

Mr. Adams carried him into the study. Priscilla and her mother followed them in, and they waited for the tears to stop so they could hear Chubby's story.

They heard it gradually. At first it seemed that everything might turn out to be Priscilla's fault. "She wouldn't let me — She said I couldn't —" was all that anyone could make out for about five minutes. Chubby's fingers pointed in his sister's direction.

Finally the story came.

"Prilly wouldn't let me play with the doll house!" Chubby sobbed. "Then she — she wouldn't even let me play with M. Chocolat." At the very thought of not being permitted to play with that splendid little pastry cook, Chubby nearly broke down again.

"I didn't know you wanted to play with him *that* much, Chubb," Priscilla said.

Chubby ignored this. "When Annie got into the doll house, and everybody was talking about kidnaping and everything, well, I just thought maybe I would kidnap M. Chocolat and maybe play with him just a little."

Also, it seemed, there was what is sometimes known as the last straw. This morning at breakfast nobody had paid much attention to Chubby's detective methods. If he had found M. Chocolat — which he had planned to do after a few days — everyone would have thought what a fine detective Chubby was.

"I really would've put him back in a few days," Chubby insisted.

"What about the black cat?" said Priscilla. She was furious with Chubby. Not only had he frightened her out of her wits. It was humiliating to be frightened out of them by a five-year-old brother.

"Oh, that was just to make it more of a mystery," said Chubby, who was beginning to feel more like himself. "The black cat was right next to M. Chocolat."

"Next to Mrs. Biggs, you mean!" Priscilla was determined to have the last word. "You're a terrible brother!" She burst into tears. It had been a difficult night. She cried and cried.

Chubby remembered something important. "But I put them back," he said apologetically. "Prilly, I did put them back! You can go see!"

Priscilla stopped crying and looked at him. "You mean that's why you came the second time?"

"Yes," Chubby confessed. "I woke up and I was sorry I did it. And I thought if I put them back after everyone was asleep no one would ever know."

"But you knew I discovered they were gone?" said Priscilla.

Chubby admitted he knew.

"Well, did it occur to you that in the morning when I told what had happened and then M.

Chocolat and the cat were back just where they belonged, everybody would think I was crazy?"

"No, I didn't think of that, Prilly, honest," said Chubby. "I'm sorry." It was comforting to Priscila to know that Chubby didn't think of *everything*.

Just then Annie, who had been sitting neglected in a corner of the hall, said "Maiyou" and leaped up on Mr. Adams' shoulder.

"Yes, Annie, just how do *you* figure in all this?" Mr. Adams said.

"I guess she didn't like Chubby acting like that," Priscilla suggested. "I guess she decided to catch him."

"Maybe she was just playing with Chubby," Mrs. Adams said. "You know how she likes feet without shoes on them."

Priscilla had a new theory. "Annie wanted everybody to know what happened. She didn't want everyone to think I was crazy. She remembered what Chubby forgot."

"Aiyou," said Annie. It sounded something like

"of course" — indeed, as much like "of course" as "aiyou" could sound.

Priscilla picked Annie up and rubbed under her chin, Annie's favorite place. "I think Annie should have an award," she announced.

"I think we'd better talk about that in the morning," said Mrs. Adams.

Chubby shyly put his hand in Priscilla's. "You forgive me, Prilly?"

"Of course," said Priscilla. She rubbed under Chubby's chin, just as she had under Annie's. Priscilla was sleepy!

"Off to bed, both of you!" Mrs. Adams commanded. The black cat chose that cheerful moment to howl. Drowsy as she was, Priscilla shivered.

"We really must try to find out whom that cat belongs to," said Mrs. Adams.

Priscilla opened her eyes wide for just a moment. "Do you think it belongs to someone?" she mumbled. "Someone real?"

The black cat replied with a low, mysterious cry.

THE
STRANGE
BLACK
CAT

## EIGHT

Tim was annoyed the next morning when he returned from Pete's and discovered that he had missed what he called "some more fun."

Priscilla had been trying to think of an "award" for Annie. "Why don't we make her her own doll house?" she said suddenly. "Will you help, Tim?"

Tim looked doubtful. 'Doesn't have to have stained-glass windows, does it?" he said. Tim always had to have his joke even if it was terrible.

When Mrs. Adams heard about Priscilla's idea, she suggested a heavy cardboard carton in the attic. "You could cut lots of windows and doors in it," she pointed out.

"And it would be nice and dark inside the way she likes!" Priscilla added.

The carton was fetched and Tim got right to

work with a certain amount of supervision from Priscilla, Chubby, and even Annie. Annie, as a matter of fact, was ready to move in before the first window was finished.

Finally, Tim had covered Annie's house with as many windows, practically, as Priscilla's. There were even windows on top. When it was finished, the children placed it in a corner of the study. Annie jumped in promptly and all that could be seen of her for at least ten minutes was a pair of shiny eyes looking out.

"Now that you've finished that little job, Tim," said Mrs. Adams, "I think you should look for that black cat. It's been around for two days. I've watched the 'Lost' ads but no one seems to be advertising for it. Perhaps we'd better put in a 'Found' ad. First, though, we'd better have the cat here in the house in case the owner should come for it."

"Probably belongs to some witch," said Tim, looking at Priscilla. "Got left behind last Halloween."

"I don't think that's very funny," said Priscilla haughtily.

Tim looked carefully at her. "Why, I do believe our Prilly thinks the animal is haunted," he teased.

Priscilla frowned. "I do *not* think it's haunted, Tim Adams," she said. "But it is, well, strange."

Nevertheless, after lunch she and Chubby joined Tim in the cat hunt. All of them went around the neighborhood calling "Kitty! Kitty!" but the only replies they received were from Annie. The black cat seemed to have vanished as mysteriously as it had arrived.

The children were sprawled in the living room discussing this disappearance when the doorbell rang. Mrs. Adams admitted a tall, pleasant-faced lady who introduced herself as Miss Winter.

"I'm so sorry to bother you," Miss Winter said, accepting a chair. "But I'm looking for a black cat. Have you seen one?"

Everybody laughed, even Priscilla. Nobody could help it. Miss Winter looked puzzled, but she understood after Mrs. Adams told about the howling stranger.

"He must be the one," Miss Winter said. "This one has a deep voice, too. That may be because he's part Siamese. Black cats often are, you know." As though in response to these comments, Annie entered the room and began sniffing Miss Winter's shoes and the hem of her dress very, very carefully.

"That's probably why the black cat had such a funny voice," said Chubby. "My, wouldn't you think we'd have recognized it? My goodness!"

Priscilla couldn't quite believe. "Of course, maybe this *isn't* your cat," she said wistfully.

Mrs. Adams ignored Priscilla. "I'm so sorry the cat doesn't seem to be here now," she said. "What led you to us?"

"I must explain that I lived next door to Mrs. Eugenia Chadwell," Miss Winter began.

"Great-aunt Eugenia!" Priscilla exclaimed.

"Yes," Miss Winters said. "Although, as you must know, she saw almost no one during the last few months of her life, she let me do her a few

little favors. She knew she wouldn't live much longer. And she asked if I would take care of her cat after she died."

Miss Winter was about to continue when the newsboy opened the Adams' screened door and tossed the evening paper in. Then suddenly, before anyone could know quite what had happened, there was bedlam.

A black streak, admitted along with the evening paper, galloped up the stairs, with Annie in hot pursuit. There were sounds of a terrible commotion — hissing and howling and every terrible noise a cat has ever been known to make.

"We'd better go up!" said Mrs. Adams. Everybody, including Miss Winter, hurried to the stairs.

When they reached the top, they rushed into Priscilla's room. There were no cats in there. The disturbance seemed to be coming from the study, and they went on down the hall.

There a strange sight met their eyes. Annie was sitting on top of her new house and the black cat was peering out of it. If there had been a fight, it appeared to be over. Nobody was hissing or howling. Two cats were sitting and looking very innocent.

"I must make Shadow a house like that," Miss Winter said. "Hi, Shadow!"

"Shadow!" cried Priscilla.

"Shadow!" said Chubby.

Priscilla told about finding the note that said, "This is the House of Shadow."

"That's right," Miss Winter said. "I believe Shadow used to sleep in the doll house. Mrs. Chadwell had odd notions at times. She put the little sign on it saying it was Shadow's house. Perhaps that explains why he climbed into the delivery truck with it."

"Oh, *that's* how he came!" Priscilla realized. "With the doll house when it was delivered!"

Miss Winter explained that she hadn't missed Shadow right away because he often went off for a day or two of prowling. Then a neighbor reported seeing Shadow in the delivery truck which had picked up the doll house.

They sat down in the study for a few moments. Shadow remained in Annie's new house, but he had his neck out and Miss Winter attached a leash to his collar.

Chubby, the great detective, now tracked down a clue which had been missing when they really needed it. "Remember when Annie first saw the doll house how she acted? Remember how she growled and arched her back and puffed up her tail?"

They all remembered.

"Well, she smelled Shadow, I bet," Chubby announced importantly.

"That's right," Mrs. Adams agreed. "And then when I put her out of the doll house, she was so busy being cross with me, and so busy trying to get back in, that she must have decided not to think about the other cat she smelled."

Priscilla looked at Shadow and then at Miss Winter. "You're sure this *is* your cat?" she said. Everyone laughed.

"I think Priscilla likes mysteries," Mrs. Adams

said. "She doesn't seem to want this one to be solved."

Priscilla had brought into the study the little black metal cat as a "doll" for Annie's doll house, but Annie had shown not a particle of interest in it. Priscilla picked it up now and examined it closely. It didn't look creepy to her any more, and its eyes didn't even look unfriendly. In fact, it was rather a cute little cat. On the other hand, Priscilla thought, it had been odd the way this little cat had kept disappearing. She didn't mention this out loud, though.

"There's often a simple explanation for the strangest things," her mother said.

"But, Mother, you said there were ghosts in Great-aunt Eugenia's house," Priscilla pointed out reproachfully.

"I said what?" Mrs. Adams asked, looking positively astounded.

"You told Cousin Julia on the phone that Great-aunt Eugenia lived in a house filled with ghosts!"

"Oh, dear, I'm sorry," Mrs. Adams said, and she couldn't quite smother a smile. "When people say a house is filled with ghosts, they generally mean it's filled with sad memories. That was all I meant!"

"Oh," said Priscilla. Then she had another thought. "What about the old Burton house at the end of the bus line? Mabel says that's *really* haunted!"

Annie decided to answer this question. "Mai-you!" she remarked. Then she rushed down the hall and they heard some strange noises from the direction of Priscilla's room.

"Better investigate," Mrs. Adams said. Priscilla, Tim, and Chubby followed her down the hall. Miss Winter and Shadow stood at a polite distance. In Priscilla's room Annie was found on the front lawn of the doll house, a paw reaching through one of the hinged windows on the second floor.

While the children watched, speechless, Annie poked her head through the bedroom window and selected something carefully with her little teeth. She jumped down and rushed from the room with it. As she went by, Priscilla recognized that Annie's prize was — Amanda! Amanda in her red dress obviously was still Annie's favorite.

"I see why she didn't mind Shadow getting into her house," Tim observed. "She still likes this one better!"

"I guess we'll have to fix those windows so they won't swing open any more," Chubby declared in his most impressive manner.

"It's strange that *Shadow* didn't try to get into this house," Priscilla said. "If it's *really* his!"

Mrs. Adams says that she has two stubborn children, Priscilla and Annie. If you want to know the truth, it's been three years since all this happened, and stubborn Annie is still trying, every so often, to force her way into Priscilla's doll house.

As for Priscilla — she has never quite given up the idea that maybe there was more to the doll house mystery than anybody ever knew.

It's certainly true that the little black metal cat disappeared after Shadow's departure, and hasn't been found to this day . . . .

This edition is published by
The Washington Dolls' House Toy Museum
5236 44th Street, N.W.
Washington, D.C. 20015